Hippo and Monkey

Hippo and Monkey

by Joshua Yunger

Download the free soundtrack for Hippo and Monkey performed
by the author at www.bunkerhillpublishing.com

www.bunkerhillpublishing.com
by Bunker Hill Publishing Inc.
285 River Road, Piermont
New Hampshire 03779, USA

10 9 8 7 6 5 4 3 2 1

Library of Congress Control Number: 2012937195

ISBN 9781593731076

Designed by Joe Lops
Printed in China

For Erin

Deep in the bright jungle, far from human ears, a hippo led what it considered to be a fairly normal life.

"I live alone in the river and on the land," said Hippo.

Hippo did have one friend in the jungle, a monkey.

Monkey didn't like the water,

and Hippo had had difficulty sitting in the trees.

But they still spent plenty of time together.

Even though Hippo and Monkey were best friends, Hippo would sometimes become annoyed with the way Monkey behaved.

Hippo would
roar and splash
water around.

Monkey usually just ignored Hippo
and continued doing monkeyish things.

"I don't like being ignored!" roared Hippo.

Soon, Hippo would lose interest in being angry
and go back to contemplating the river and the land.

After a time, ignoring Hippo's regular outbursts became difficult for Monkey.

Being very clever,

Monkey hatched a plan.

Traveling quickly

by vine . . .

Monkey was in an area inhabited

by humans in a short time.

Monkey waited until the humans were gone and then carefully borrowed a piece of the river that Monkey had often seen the humans examine themselves with.

Monkey kept the river sliver hidden until . . .

Hippo began to throw his body back and forth in the water and roar with teeth showing, apparently in reaction to some monkeyish thing.

At this time, Monkey took the shimmering yet seemingly dead piece of water out of hiding.

Monkey held it
up to Hippo and
stood behind it.

Hippo saw in the mirror all the commotion
he was making and stopped.

"I do very hippoish things," he said,
"just like Monkey does her monkeyish things,
except I am being far more obnoxious
than Monkey ever was."

Hippo didn't stop roaring or shaking around
in the water because it was kind of fun . . .

but Hippo never again roared at Monkey,

and Monkey never again ignored Hippo.

The End